GW00857721

WOMEN
IN
SHORTS

stories and monologues

by

Jenefer Heap

First published in 2017

www.jeneferheap.wordpress.com

ISBN-10: 1979054959
ISBN-13: 978-1979054959

This book is dedicated to my mother

Molly Rosser

and all the women in shorts

Also by Jenefer Heap

The Woman Who Never Did

Contents

FAB at 50

Oh. My. God. What are they all doing here? Mum and Dad, Jeff and the twins, Tina and Christine from the bank. Purple balloons ...

And a banner – 'FAB AT 50'. Oh please. Oh no. No no no no! There's Penny from the hairdressers – I told her I was forty-five.

What's my face doing? Smile mouth, smile! Eyes, try to keep up! Oh My God, it's the whole Pilates class.

'Robin! What a ... lovely ... surprise, darling. How did you keep it a secret?'

How indeed? Emily must have helped him – quite the Little Miss Organiser these days, juggling her career and her family. She mightn't find it quite such a breeze without my unpaid childminding and freezer filling.

And did I or did I not specifically tell them that I loathe surprise parties?

Thank God, a drink at last.

'Emily, darling. Did you and Daddy arrange all of this? How clever of you!'

Just hand over the damn champagne.

Do I really know all these people? Where did they dredge them up from? Is that Lawrence? I thought he was dead.

Janette's looking amazing – mind you she's had work done. And her Brian earns a fortune. That dress alone cost more than my annual clothes budget.

Oh My God. What am I wearing? Robin said we were just going out for a quiet meal at the pub. I've got my old coat on – I was walking the dog in it this morning. These jeans aren't too clean either. At least I'm wearing my pink cashmere. But I haven't even had my roots done. Still, I see my beloved daughter and her brood have all got new outfits. And Robin had a trim this afternoon. How could they do this to me?

'Alice, darling, and Charles … Wonderful to see you! How are the boys? Oh, they're here too!'

How many people have they invited? It must have cost a fortune. You could get a nice little diamond for this kind of money. Or Robin could have whisked me off to a tropical paradise. And what do I get? A party I don't want. Oh, yes, and a scruffy little wooden box. What did he call it – an antique puzzle box? More like a mangy old second-hand Rubik's cube.

Thank God they had the sense to get the pub to do the catering. Imagine playing hostess to this lot at home. With Emily in the kitchen we'd all have spent the night in A&E – either third degree burns or food poisoning. I can see the headlines now 'Salmonella in the South Downs' and a nice picture of me throwing up in front of that wretched banner.

Mum and Dad have had too much to drink already. We'll have to send them home in a taxi. Robin's parents too by the look of it. I hope they're not driving back to Dorset tonight.

'Hello, Joan. Clive. Lovely to see you both. Oops! Steady there!'

Just as I thought.

'Yes, hasn't he been clever. I never knew he was so devious.'

But I know now, Robin, and I won't forget in a hurry.

'Reverend! How good of you to come!'

Thank the Lord! A chance to escape the in-laws.

'Yes, isn't he a sweetheart. And my daughter too. I'm doubly blessed. No, I haven't seen the cake yet. Rather special you say?'

Oh. My. God. That's my photograph on the cake – eighteen months old and naked in a washing up bowl. And who'd have thought they'd fit fifty candles around the outside.

'Robin!'

He's wittering on about that damn box again. A little challenge – if I solve it I win a prize. If I want a challenge, Robin, I'll do a Sudoku. If I want a prize, I'll buy a lottery ticket – aim just a little higher than a family of woodworm.

There's a tableful of presents at the back of the room. It'll be the usual rubbish: body lotion and soap I'd never choose, scarves in the wrong colour and someone else's idea of a good read. I'll be writing thank you cards for weeks! Wait a minute though … What's that …? Are those suitcases under the table? He's taking me away somewhere after all! Oh, Robin, you darling!

Uh-oh – the in-laws are back.

'What was that, Joan? For a week? Two whole weeks? With us? How … lovely. So those are your cases?'

Oh My God. That's why Robin offered to hoover the spare room.

'Excuse me a moment. Bit stuffy in here – I just need some fresh air.'

Menopausal woman coming through. Hot flushes. Volatile emotional state!

'Hello, Lawrence. Lovely to see you. And looking so well.'

Oh get out of my way – I need a cigarette! My own sodding party and I have to go out in the rain for a smoke.

Where's my lighter? I can't find anything in my bag except that wretched box. Why on earth did Robin insist I bring it?

'Maureen. You life saver! I was gasping.'

Inhale ... and ... out. That's better, I can breathe again.

At least it's quiet out here. Just the soothing pitter-patter of the rain on the smoking shelter roof. Clear my head a bit ...

Oh My God! It's Maureen's birthday tomorrow. I'd completely forgotten and one of those gifts is bound to be from her ...

I know! Maureen can have the box.

'Happy Birthday for tomorrow, Maureen!'

Her house is full of old tat.

'You love it? I'm so pleased – I thought of you as soon as I saw it.'

I'll tell Robin I lost it – serve him right.

'Taxi? Must you be off so soon? Oh. The Seychelles. Tonight. For your birthday. I didn't realise it was a special one ... Oh. It isn't ... Just a little treat from your Norman.'

Deep, deep breath.

'How ... lovely. Well, off you go now. You don't want to miss that plane. Bye, Maureen ...'

... and sod you Maureen. And sod this cheap champagne, I need a brandy. Oh My God. Here comes Emily again, all smiles and giggles.

'What's that, darling? Have I found my sparkly prize?'

Sparkly?

'You want me to have another go at that puzzle box? Darling, you know I'm no good at that sort of thing.'

5

Sparkly prize?

'It's supposed to be a secret. But I need to try because Daddy's put something very special inside …'

Oh. My. God.

A Change of Address

Elspeth wrote her new address very carefully on the last of the invitations. It wouldn't do to make a mistake.

She'd already finished her 'change of address' cards. Just the one small pack; so many family and friends had lost touch over the years. As for her neighbours – well, it would be a relief to see the back of them.

It had seemed such an idyllic village at first. A wonderful opportunity to transplant her world-weary roots from the concrete anonymity of town to the neighbourly soil of the English countryside. But beneath that chocolate box facade lurked a far less palatable reality. Elspeth had tried her best: turned out for church every Sunday morning, volunteered in the community café, and offered advice to the Neighbourhood Watch. But she hadn't been invited to join so much as a book group, despite her hints about being such an avid reader. Just two years after moving in, she was moving on.

Elspeth took a sip of coffee and glanced out of the kitchen window, the view of her pretty garden blighted by the four-by-four looming above the hollyhocks. Next door were parked across her frontage again – so selfish and all to avoid walking an extra few yards to their door. Such a difficult couple. She had tried reasoning with them, but the whole affair had resulted in a flurry of nasty letters around the village – some of them anonymous and written in angry purple ink.

In recent years, Elspeth had been plagued by parking problems – people always took advantage of a widow. She'd virtually been forced out of her previous house in town. Such a genteel neighbourhood, until that family moved in opposite with their three cars, not one of them respectably shut away in the garage, and not once had she seen the husband out there with a chamois. Then the house next door was let to students, each driving some noisy old rust-bucket. It came to something, Elspeth thought bitterly, when a lady of advancing years, and not in the best of health, couldn't park on the road outside her own house. Even her Good Neighbour Campaign, designed to shame them all into being more considerate, had taken a most unpleasant turn. And then to discover she'd moved to such an unwelcoming … Well, the sooner she moved on, the better.

But Elspeth was confident she'd chosen wisely at last. Such a charming house; she could just picture her little white hatchback in its own numbered parking bay. An exclusive retirement development on the outskirts of a smart little market town. The residents would be of a certain maturity and financial status – no battered old cars. And everyone would be a new neighbour – no smug little cliques to navigate.

Elspeth was also much better prepared. She'd made a plan of the parking allocation for each house and she'd almost finished the invitations to the inaugural meeting of the Neighbourhood Watch – a meeting she would both host and chair herself.

Outside Elspeth's kitchen window her elderly neighbour limped slowly to his car, supported by his equally elderly wife. What business did a man of that age and infirmity have with a four-by-four anyway?

Elspeth turned her back on them, signing her name on the last invitation – in dark purple ink.

On the Way Home

Mummy'd stopped shouting, but her face was still red and cross. She was holding me too tight – my sleeve and a pinchy bit of skin. I wanted her to cuddle me, but she wouldn't let go my arm and she was hanging onto Douglas's hood with her other hand.

Two old ladies with posh coats and fat tummies were staring. The purple one said 'Tut' and the green one said 'It's a shame'.

Mummy told them to 'Bugger Off!'

Then Douglas shouted 'ugga goff!' and they did.

Mummy shouted at the man in the horrible car too.

'You Could've Killed Her, You Moron!'

'Teach Your Kids Some Road Sense, You Stupid Cow!'

I wanted to tell him I do Kerbsafe at school. But I dropped Mummy's flower I made to cheer her up. And I forgot about Kerbsafe.

We were on the way home and there were lots of cars and I had to be a Clever Big Girl because Mummy was carrying two bags of shopping AND holding Douglas's hand AND he was waving his Monkey around and being wriggly. I don't like the noise and the bright lights when it's getting dark. I don't really like cars much, except Daddy's when I'm safe in the back.

I was trying to keep up and not get in everyone's way. When Mummy started crossing the road, I was right behind her. But I dropped the flower. Then the horrible car squealed and tooted. And Mummy grabbed me. And I fell over the kerb. And all the shouting started.

'You Stupid Stupid Girl! Never Never Stop When You're Crossing The Road!'

Then she shouted at the horrible car man and the old ladies.

After they'd all gone, Mummy and me picked up the shopping. I really wanted a cuddle, but she had her hands full of shopping bags and Douglas. So I gave Mummy a cuddle instead because she was crying – very quietly so only we two knew.

Then Douglas said, 'Where Monkey?' and I saw his Monkey lying in the road and cars driving over it.

Mummy said, 'Lily, keep hold of Douglas.'

And then she held up her hand to stop the traffic. All the cars tooted and everyone stared, but she just walked out into the road to rescue Monkey.

Douglas said, 'Poor Monkey. Daddy fix him.'

I looked at Mummy and wondered if she'd tell him. And she did at last.

'Daddy's gone, Douglas. Mummy and Lily will give Monkey a wash and mend him and he'll be good as new by bedtime.'

We held hands the rest of the way home. Douglas in the middle and Mummy and me on the outside. It didn't matter we were in the way, everyone walked round us.

Mummy said, 'Sorry, Lily. Thank you for being my Clever Big Girl.'

And that was nearly as good as a cuddle.

Zigzag Lines

He's looking out the window at me again. Him at number forty-three. I'm only doing my job, aren't I? Buy a house near a school and you're going to have trouble with parking. You've got to expect it.

Still, at least he hasn't said anything. Not like the other week. Oh he was horrible, and him a big strapping chap in his prime. I'm seventy-five, you know. I'm told I don't look it, but I am. Seventy-five and still out here twice a day. Eight-thirty till nine to see them safely in. Then back again at three to see them safely out again.

Where was I? Oh yes, the other week. Wednesday afternoon I think it was. I was just getting ready for the early bird mums. You know, the clucky ones who think their chicks can't manage a few hours without them, and the dashing about ones in a hurry to grab their kiddies and drive them off to tap classes or tennis coaching or whatnot. I'd fetched my lollipop from the staffroom and as I came out the school gates there he was, charging across the road. Red in the face and shouting the odds at me about all the cars and the new zigzag lines. How I was infringing his human rights and he couldn't park outside his house anymore. As if I'd painted them myself when he wasn't looking. It's taken long enough for us to get them. All the other schools round here had them ages ago, and even now the council have only done it as a trial. Besides, they only overlap his house a few yards. Anyway, I started to explain all calmly about the safety assessment and that little lad in Reception nearly getting knocked down just before half term and how the teachers can't see round his van when they're coming out the school gates into traffic.

Well, you should've heard what he called me. I've never been spoken to like that. None of the kiddies would be so rude, not even the big ones who've left and gone to high school and think they know it all. Not even they would speak to me like that. He was worse than the lot of them – the language! And he must be a foot taller than me.

Now I may be getting on a bit, but I'm no shrinking violet. Never have been, never will be. Well you couldn't be, not in a job like this. You have to be able to stand your ground when the four-by-fours come honking down the hill. And when those parents who only live round the corner leave their cars up on the pavement. Oh, I've heard all their excuses: 'I know I shouldn't, June, but it's just for a moment, honestly and I've got a meeting at half past nine in Cirencester'. It's all part and parcel of this job. So, I stood my ground in front of that big bully of a man. And I kept my manners too, even if he didn't. I told him those zigzag lines were just on a trial, we were going to review it in a week. I tried to explain it was nothing personal, but the kiddies' safety had to come first and that he should know that, even if he didn't have any kiddies himself.

Oh, he got really mad then. Came right up close, he did. I took a tight hold on my lollipop in case I needed to defend myself. My knees were all wobbly. I thought they were going to give way and I'd end up sat down, right there on the pavement

Well, that's when the mums started arriving. First, I heard was someone call across the road: 'You all right, June?' It was Sam's mum, her that works in the Golden Lion.

Then Georgie's mum. 'Is something the matter here?' and she came over and stood right next to me.

Then Poppy J's mum and Poppy W's. And soon there was quite a little group. All those mums standing shoulder to shoulder with me. All staring at that great big angry bully.

Well, the coward just turned tail, marched straight back in his house and shut the door. Someone fetched me a glass of water and a couple of the mums stayed with me while we waited for the children to come out. They could see I was upset.

Poppy W's mum put her arm round me. 'You should call the police, June,' she said. 'Make a formal complaint. We'll all back you up.'

'Shall I get Phil to go round and have a word?' Sam's mum chipped in. 'He needs sorting out.'

Georgie's mum put her hand on my arm. 'I'm sure there's no need for that,' she said. 'He's just got himself all worked up. When he calms down he'll be thoroughly ashamed of himself, June. I'm sure he'll apologise.'

And then they all started fussing and saying I should have a lie down. Well, I told them I didn't want a fuss and I drank my glass of water and just got on with it. Thank you very much, I told them. I'm very grateful for your support. But I'm feeling much better now and I'm certainly not going to neglect my job because of some silly man who ought to know better than harassing a woman in her seventies who's just doing her bit for the community. And then I picked up my lollipop and showed those kiddies across the road.

Georgie's mum was wrong, he hasn't apologised. But he hasn't come near me since. Doesn't dare to when the mums are around. Just glares at me from his window. I haven't been to the police, though. I've decided to rise above it.

Besides, I've had my hands full getting my report together. About the zig-zag lines. My supervisor's coming this afternoon for an interim review. See how the trial's been going. 'Have they made a positive improvement?' she wants to know. 'Are they sufficient?'

Well, I'll be pleased to report that they certainly have made a positive improvement. It's much easier to see up and down the road with the space near school kept clear. But are they sufficient? Well, I'm afraid I'm going to have to tell her no, sadly I don't think they are. I reckon those zig-zag lines need to extend about another ten yards. Right across the front of number forty-three.

Angela

We just got talking at the hairdressers. 'As you do,'
Angela said. Although, to be honest, it isn't something
I usually do. Once upon a time, perhaps, but these
days I tend to keep myself to myself.

We sat down at adjacent mirrors. I was just having
a wet cut, but Angela was having the works: colour,
cut and blow dry. It was only my second time at the
salon, but I'd seen Angela there before, although she
didn't remember me. 'I'm their best customer,' she
told me. 'Every fourth Thursday. They understand my
hair so well – why risk a stranger?'

Angela was excited that afternoon and she wanted
an audience. The salon wasn't busy so, even though I
was finished, I stayed put in the chair to oblige. Her
daughter was coming home that evening after almost

twenty-six months in hospital and rehab. A car crash. 'Had to be cut from the wreckage,' Angela said. 'According to the doctors she should never have survived. But she's a stubborn woman, my daughter – never one to follow other people's rules.' Angela listed the surgeries and specialists and how they had to teach her to walk again. 'Now she's coming home at last – I can't stop talking about it,' she said. Which was true. I couldn't get a word in. But that was fine by me.

I also heard all about Angela's grandson. She'd been looking after him while his mother was recovering. I think she assumed I was a pensioner too, because she asked if I had any grandchildren. Actually, I'm a lot younger than I look, but I've gone very grey over the last couple of years and I don't really follow fashion or bother much with make-up. Dull hair, dull clothes, no lipstick – the invisible woman. Which suits me very well.

Angela was quite the opposite: groomed and glamorous, glowing with confidence and happiness. But she and I were a good match that afternoon. She wanted to talk and I know how to listen. I like to stock up on other people's lives: their highs, their lows. I replay the details when I can't get to sleep, when my head is full of 'how things might have turned out differently'. It was easy listening to Angela, all I had to do was to smile and make occasional murmuring noises. Her excitement was infectious, the whole salon was buzzing with it, but the flow was interrupted by a fanfare of electronic music – Angela's mobile phone.

She pulled it out of her handbag. A shocking pink case embellished with a diamante 'AB'.

'Yes,' she purred. 'Mrs Angela Beresford. The Merc. Yes.' Then her voice changed. 'But that's completely unacceptable. I need it for the school run. I have to pick my grandson up. It's particularly important that I'm on time today.'

My hatchback was parked just outside and I had nothing else to do that afternoon. Yet I hesitated. But not for long. I watched as Angela sent a text to her grandson telling him to look out for a different car. She had one of those smart phones, the latest model I expect, but I don't really know. I don't own a mobile phone these days. Can't stand the things.

'How lucky we met!' said Angela.

On the way to the school, I dropped a few hints. I was a widow too. No, I didn't have a daughter, but there had been a son. Angela was so full of her own plans she didn't pick up on what I was saying, although she tutted sympathetically when I mentioned the accident. That they, my husband and my son, they too had to be cut from the wreckage of their car. Angela didn't ask how long ago it had happened. And I didn't tell her.

Nor did I mention the woman who drove into the back of the van that was travelling too close to the car in front and rammed it into the oncoming traffic. A six-car pileup caused by a woman who thought the rules didn't apply to her. A woman fiddling with her smart phone. Probably answering a call from her mother.

I took a couple of wrong turnings, so we arrived at the school a few minutes late, long enough for the crowds of children to disperse. Angela was getting twitchy, but her grandson was waiting on the corner when we arrived. He looked about eleven. My son was ten.

All I had to do was press down hard on the accelerator.

But my legs began to shake. I stalled the car.

'Ooops-a-daisy!' said Angela. 'You ought to get a Merc, they're very reliable. And safe too – my daughter would probably have died if she'd been driving a cheaper car.'

She called her grandson over. 'Hello, darling. This is … oooh, I never caught your name.'

The boy climbed into the back seat, prattling on about his day at school and his mother's homecoming. Angela and her grandson left no airspace in the conversation for me. It didn't matter, the only sounds I could hear clearly were the thumping of my heart in my chest and the pulsing of my blood between my temples. All I could think was: I could have done it. I almost did.

Now I'm lying here, unable to sleep. But I have plenty to think about.

Not just about Angela: her highs and lows; the big day she's had today; how much she talked and how little she listened. Tonight, I will also let my head fill with thoughts of 'how things might have turned out differently'.

Tomorrow I will call the hairdressers. And book myself in for a trim in four weeks' time.

Daisy Dances

It is early evening in the garden. That magic hour – after tea, not quite bath time, not quite bed time. Daisy is making the most of the last of the spring sunshine, the end of her day. Her plump toes sink into the sun-warmed grass as she dances round and round the apple tree. She is wearing her fairy outfit. Mummy's lilac scarf floats gracefully over a pink vest that is spotted with ketchup and yoghurt. Pink paper wings (the glue still a little wet) bob up and down on her back. A trail of glitter and sequins leads back to the kitchen door – really-truly fairy dust from the kit they made this afternoon.

From the doorway, Sarah can see her daughter is completely absorbed in the dance. If she listens carefully, she can hear Daisy humming to the music playing in her head and singing out instructions to her companions: a tiger, a unicorn and a talking bear. As she sings, Daisy waves her glittery wand in smooth but intricate patterns over each animal's head. The tiger is so fast that she has to run around in circles to keep up. The unicorn is so tall, that the wand catches in the branches and a shower of late blossom sprinkles the dancers with pink petals. When she comes to the talking bear, Daisy pauses in her dance, whispering in his ear and nodding solemnly over their shared confidences.

Sarah finishes her chores and brings her cup of tea out into the garden. She sighs as she remembers a very different Daisy at nursery school this morning: a shy little girl who longed to play with the other children, but stayed in the shadows by the back wall until it was time to go home. The curse of the only child who doesn't understand the rules and can't yet summon the confidence for their noisy games. It will come. It has to come. Daisy is bright and courageous, but it's a hard lesson to learn.

The sun is lower now, shining through the chestnut trees that grow along the track leading to the village. The garden is striped with long shadows and a brightness that lights her child with a golden glow. Sarah is warmed by love for her fairy girl, love mingled with sadness that the moment will soon be gone and the fairy lost forever. She paints the picture in her memory, this dear little person with her golden curls and paper wings. Her very own home-made fairy – ketchup stains and all.

In the clarity of the early evening light she can almost glimpse Daisy's companions as they dance on the grass. Sarah smiles. They are a lively bunch, good company and mostly well-behaved – although sometimes the tiger gets a bit rough, and the bear can be sharp-tongued. Daisy need never be lonely when she has such an imagination. The sunlight shifts again and, just for a moment, Sarah sees a shade, an echo of her own childhood high among the blossom. A little girl cradling a tiny dragon, hiding it from the scrutiny of her own, rather matter-of-fact, parents. A little girl who is learning to play at last.

Across the garden, Daisy stops beneath the tree. Looks up into its branches, her head tilted to one side. Then she runs across the grass towards her mother.

'Mummy, Mummy, come and dance.'

Ticking

In retrospect, the thing with Al was pretty predictable. He was over from the States. We were working together on a major project, high profile stuff. He was in charge of finance, I was in the change facilitation team. Long hours, mega stress levels, people get close in these situations.

Everybody liked Al, he was the all American nice guy and good for a laugh too. In many ways, we were from pretty different worlds, but it felt like we had a lot in common, so I played down the mismatches. Like the difference in our backgrounds – he was from a mid-West farming family and my dad was the manager of a high street building society in Kidderminster. And the difference in our ages – Al was, technically speaking, old enough to be my father, but we joked about that. Besides which, his energy and his attitude to life certainly didn't seem to belong to a man in his fifties. As for what we both wanted out of life? Well we didn't get around to discussing that. Not at the time.

For months we'd been getting sort of flirty at work, but keeping it professional. Then, all of a sudden, Al's assignment was coming to an end and he announced he was off in a week's time to manage a new department at the Paris office. I suppose I just thought it was 'now or never'. I'd been in a kind of on-off relationship with a guy who worked in IT, but it wasn't really going anywhere and time was ticking on. So, I set the whole thing up: Al and I were both going to a drinks party to mark the project's second phase go-live, and I made sure I was on hand to drive him back to his apartment to continue the celebrations in private. Then later, much later, I drove back to my place for a quick shower and change before work. It was good – very, very good. Al combined the experience and repertoire of his years, with the energy and enthusiasm of a much younger man. Better than good, it was amazing. And it was obviously pretty amazing for Al too, because we managed to fit in two more dates before he had to leave for Paris.

I was desperate to see him again. So, imagine my excitement when I got the phone call, less than a fortnight later. Al's new department needed help with their change management programme – to help their graduate trainee, Marie-Nicole, get up to speed. He'd told everyone I was the best in my field – could I come over for a couple of days? And why not stay the weekend and soak up a bit of Parisian culture?

What an amazing time. Saturday afternoon we explored Montmartre, enjoying the Arty atmosphere and having our portraits sketched in pastels – Al even had them framed. On Sunday morning, we moseyed around the flea markets on the Rive Gauche and Al fell in love with a scantily clad Venus on a gilded ormolu clock. That night, we listened to it ticking away in pride of place on his mantelpiece and I teased him for paying over the odds without even haggling. Al pulled me close, looked deep into my eyes, and said that he would have paid twice the amount because he wanted this beautiful lady all to himself – he couldn't bear the thought of any other man touching her.

Next thing I knew, the Paris office needed me on a monthly basis – always a Friday or Monday so that I could stop over on the weekend for a bit of culture.

Of course, I was swept along by the glamour of it all. Once a month, Al would meet me at Charles de Gaulle in his sports car, champagne on ice back at his corporate apartment with views of the Champs-Élysées. All just a short walk from the best nightlife Paris could offer. Al took me to the top places – not that we ever went out on my first night, we were way too busy. I'd spend a few hours in the office with Marie-Nicole, but the rest of the time was a rosy blur of Michelin star restaurants, fantastic sex, and champagne breakfasts in bed, all with a beautiful Parisian backdrop. One long luscious weekend every month.

We had to be discrete, of course. All those business trips mightn't have looked good to the internal auditors. And so it went on: Spring afternoons by the Seine; Summer sunsets from the steps of the Sacré-Cœur; Autumn walks through the Tuileries; and cosy Winter evenings making love by the fire in Al's apartment, lying in the afterglow listening to the tick-tick of the ormolu clock.

Almost two and a half wonderful years. More than enough time, more than enough romance, to get my imagination working overtime. All those things we'd never talked about. Settling down together – maybe we'd marry, maybe we wouldn't – it wasn't important, after all Al had been married twice before. The different places we might live – Paris, the U.K., maybe even Al's family farm. And babies, of course there would be babies – Al loved babies, he already had two grown up daughters, and a couple of granddaughters too.

Then one night, as I was packing my bag ready to fly to Paris the next day, I looked up at my portrait from Montmartre, hanging above the bed (I always found it strange that Al kept his shut away in the spare room) and realised that, once again, it was 'now or never'. The Paris assignment might be over in a few months and that would be the end of our romantic weekends. Time was ticking on. Indeed, for me, now almost thirty-eight, my biological clock was ticking on. Loud and clear as Al's ormolu.

The gilded Venus still featured prominently on his mantelpiece, but it was no longer centre stage, having been joined by a dozen other iconic European antiques: glassware, carvings, even a clockwork bear. Al's collection – I should have picked up on that. Was I really anything more than another souvenir of his authentic European experience? The English Rose scattering her petals across his king-sized bed.

But all I could hear was the ticking. It must have sent me a little crazy, winding up my imagination. I imagined getting 'accidentally' pregnant: Al's initial shock, his determination to 'do the right thing', how hard I'd work to gain the acceptance of his family, then his joy as I handed him the son he'd never had. I even imagined it would be a good idea to talk all this through with Al that weekend.

Of course, things didn't work out quite like that. Al, who was already paying two lots of alimony from two failed marriages and planning how to fund an early retirement with enough spare cash for membership at the golf-club and holidays in the Caribbean, had different plans for his future.

Marie-Nicole was suddenly promoted to Change Facilitation Co-ordinator, so there was no longer any need for my monthly visits. She sent me a charming email, full of appreciation of the help she'd received from this older, far more experienced, woman. I immediately pressed Delete, wondering if Marie-Nicole had taken on any of my other roles and responsibilities.

That last weekend I spent with Al seemed cruelly drawn-out without the pretence of a rosy future. He remained the all American nice guy to the end, but I lay awake each night, my heart raw and exposed, listening to the hours tick by till the morning. By the time he drove me to the airport, we were both counting down the minutes. I told him there was no need to wait, kissed him on the cheek and said something corny, like 'Have a nice life, Al'. Then I turned and walked off. I didn't, I couldn't, look back.

I'll never forget the flight home. Face pressed to that cold little window to hide my tears and cool my burning face. The disappointment. The humiliation. But, mostly, the wasted time. When I closed my eyes, all I could see was the ormolu clock. And, even above the roar of the plane's engines, I could hear it tick-tick-ticking.

That Hat

'Oh,' said May's sister, Anna. '*That* hat. I thought you meant the trilby I gave you for Christmas.'

'The trilby's very … very … Smart. I know,' May replied. 'It's very *Anna*. But this hat is more May. Don't you think?'

'Oh yes. Definitely more you than me. But that's not the point. You're dressing for an interview. You want to look smart. You need to look more like me. A sensible look for a sensible job, remember.' She sighed. 'So that you can pay the rent. The money Grandma left you won't last forever, you know.'

May didn't like to tell her sister that Grandma's money was already all but gone. She frowned down at what she was wearing. 'But the rest of me does look like you. Skirt and blouse. Smart black shoes. And your little grey jacket – I'm virtually monochrome.'

Anna's phone buzzed and she glanced at the screen. 'All right,' she said. 'But hang it up as soon as you get there. For Heaven's sake, don't take it into the interview room. And don't forget a brush to tidy your hat-hair.' She picked up her bag. 'Got to dash. Tabitha's violin grading at ten thirty-five.'

May watched her sister neatly sidestep the recycling box. She sighed as Anna slid into the driving seat of her new cabriolet, elegantly swinging her pristine stilettoes inside – all of which she accomplished without the need to smooth (or tidy in any way at all) her tailored ivory jacket and pencil skirt.

After waving her off, May closed the front door and checked the hall clock, mentally adjusting the time by twelve minutes, as usual. She would buy a new clock with her first pay packet. Something efficient and reliable, the sort Anna would buy. She'd need one now she was settling down to a sensible job and a proper, grown-up life. May pictured such a clock: steel face and hands, with no nonsense numbers in a serious, serifless font. Her existing hall clock was shaped like a brightly coloured wooden parrot with only the 3 and the 7 still in situ. She'd bought it at a street market in Tierra del Fuego and carried it in her backpack for nearly four years as she took the long way home, leaving the missing digits scattered across South America.

THAT HAT

May checked her reflection in the hall mirror. The hat echoed the colours of her parrot clock: bright green with a band of pink, blue and orange, embellished with embroidered flowers of red and yellow. Anna had a point, it did look a bit odd on top of all that grey and black. Perhaps she should reconsider.

A brooch shaped like a big pink peony lay on a shelf beside the mirror. May pinned it to Anna's grey jacket. Then she pulled an orange and green scarf from the hall stand and hung it around her neck. She buckled a turquoise belt around her waist. Finally, she stepped out of the expensive black shoes and laced up her yellow biker boots.

'Much better,' smiled May. And, kicking the recycling box out of her way, she set off to catch the bus.

Tina Parker's Dad's New Car

I'd never have recognised Tina Parker if she hadn't been standing next to her mum. Well, everybody looks much the same at a funeral: same black clothes, same soggy handkerchiefs and dampness around the eyes. I wheeled Dad over to offer his condolences to Mrs Parker and there was Tina at her mother's side. I stayed in the background, shifting uncomfortably in court shoes that pinched and a skirt that no-longer fitted around my waist – clothing that hadn't seen the light of day since the last time I was at a funeral.

I held up Dad's big black umbrella, as they talked about the old days when he and Mr Parker were the stalwarts of the Lions' Club. I swapped the umbrella to my left hand to give my right arm a rest, and they moved the conversation on to Mum's eventual surrender to cancer five years ago and Mr Parker's fatal heart attack on the bowling green.

I kept my eyes busy: the floral tributes, the sign that spelled out West Wilbury Crematorium, the herringbone pattern of the block paving. I looked everywhere, anywhere except at the Parkers. Until I could no longer ignore the fact that Tina Parker was staring at me.

I took a deep breath. 'I was so sorry to hear about your father.'

She looked at me, lips subtracted, face as pale as the order of service, a dour, matronly figure. I know we all change with age, but I would never have recognised Tina Parker.

It was getting on for fifty years since we'd last met. August 1969. Last Sunday of the summer holidays. No rain that day, not a cloud in the sky. The world was as shining as our new colour TV: green grass, blue sky, mums and children in bright summer clothes, dads in their cricket whites. I felt pretty and grown-up in my psychedelic mini dress, the one Nan made from a McCalls pattern.

I was bursting to go, so I headed off to a concrete hut by the car park. The smell of poo and wee crawled to meet me. There was a single cracked window, brown with scum, and grey cobwebs crept from a hole where the lock should have been. My tummy cringed. I prodded the door open with the tip of my fingernail. Felt the dark stink within.

Tina called over. 'I wouldn't go in there if I were you.' She slid off the bonnet of her dad's new car, a redheaded stick insect in a green t-shirt, and yellow hot pants, vivid and startling against the bright white shining paintwork. 'There's shit on the floor and a huge, hairy spider – biggest I've ever seen!'

'I don't really need to go.' I replied, casually as I could.

'Come and race then.'

Tina was a make-do friend. Her dad and mine were in the Lions. I saw her at cricket matches, bonfire night, the children's Christmas party – which was always brilliant with loads of delicious food and party games and presents from one of the dads dressed up as Santa. Tina and I got along OK. She was very good at running. I wasn't, especially when I was bursting. But I wanted to play. The other girls were too young and silly for a nine-year old to bother with while the boys were all busy being Neil Armstrong and said girls weren't allowed on the moon.

'In a minute.' I called back to Tina. 'I need to see my mum.'

Mum was in the pavilion, making sandwiches and listening to the other mums complaining about their husbands. I fidgeted at her, too embarrassed to say what was wrong out loud.

'Not now, Jane. Ask Alison.'

My sister was sunbathing on an old striped rug, her long brown hair a curtain around her teen magazine.

'Go away, maggot'.

I couldn't even see Dad. He was probably fielding, but all the players looked much the same in their cricket whites.

'Race you to that tree. Ready Steady Go!' Tina sprinted off and I lumbered after her, trying to run with my knees together, tripping over my feet.

'You're hopeless!' she scoffed.

'I don't feel well.' My back was shivery hot and cold, my legs full and heavy. 'I don't want to race.'

Tina thought for a moment. 'I've got Dad's car keys. We can listen to the radio.'

I followed with careful steps, my bum tight as a new clasp purse.

The car was still shiny and smelt plastic and new. Tina jumped in. 'Let's play cops and robbers.'

She turned on the radio and sang along about Honky Tonk Women and Never Falling in Love Again, pretending to swing the wheel from side to side. I sat very still in the passenger seat clenching my thighs together. Pretending to play. Trying not to think. Looking out the window. Looking anywhere. Looking at ... that hut.

It came as Tina leapt from the car yelling, 'Quick! They're getting away – come on Danno!' A trickle. A flood. Hot smelling of summer hedges and strange flowers. I might have tried to stop. But I didn't. I sat in Tina's dad's new car and squeezed out the last drop.

Tina was away across the field shooting robbers. She'd left the driver's door wide open. I got out of the car. My dress was wet and cold, my cheeks wet and hot. I closed the passenger door, but not the driver's – perhaps they'd think it was a dog. Then I ran and ran. I kept running until my dress dried in the hot August sun. I stayed away from Tina. I played with the infants and waved the Apollo boys off to the moon until it was time to go home.

I tried not to think of Mr Parker's new car. Or Mrs Parker in the passenger seat. Or the door that Tina left open and I didn't close.

1969. For the rest of that year I found excuses to avoid the Lions Club events. I missed out on bonfire night and even feigned flu-like symptoms that kept me from the children's Christmas party. The next year we moved away and I hadn't seen Tina since, although Dad kept in touch with her dad through the Lions. Almost fifty years ago. No wonder I didn't recognise this grey haired, grey faced woman in her black dress.

'You two used to play together,' Dad said suddenly.

'But that was such a long time ago,' I added quickly. 'Tina probably doesn't remember me.'

Tina Parker looked at me for a very long moment. 'Oh yes, Jane,' she said, 'I remember.'

The Biscuit Tin

'Barb! I can't find the tin, Barb!'

Barbara looked up from the box of crockery she was unpacking. She'd been waiting for that shout. Tensed up, anticipating. She stood up stiffly, balancing a milk jug on top of a pile of crumpled newspapers, and stretched her back; the crunching in her shoulders a reminder of long days bent over boxes and crates.

She coaxed her aching joints over to the bottom of the stairs.

'It'll turn up, Fred,' she called. 'I'll put the kettle on, love. It's about time we had our tea. Beans on toast do you?'

Without waiting for an answer, Barbara went to find the toaster.

She felt her husband's presence in the doorway and heard the familiar anxiety building in his voice.

'I can't find it anywhere, Barb.'

With her back to the room, Barbara carefully cut two slices of wholemeal bread.

'We'll have a look later, love. I'll look with you.' She forced a little laugh. 'The beans have gone walkabout too. It'll have to be toast and jam.'

'I thought you packed it with your jewellery. You always pack it with your jewellery.'

Barbara filled the kettle, then lingered by the kitchen sink, staring out into the garden of yet another new home, their third in as many years, fixing her gaze on a little Japanese maple, the earth around its roots neatly patted down. 'Looks like it's going to be a lovely evening. Why don't we leave the unpacking for today, Fred? Go for a walk after tea.'

'I've emptied all the boxes in the bedroom. But it's not there.'

Still facing the window, Barbara closed her eyes, imagined the chaos upstairs, the bed strewn with clothes and bits of jewellery spilling onto the floor. She took a deep breath and turned to face her husband.

His eyes were drowning in un-spilt tears, his short grey hair sticking up in tufts where he'd worried at it as he'd searched. Barbara held out her arms and Fred stumbled towards her, stooping to rest his head on her slender shoulder. Barbara stroked his hair, tidying it with gentle fingers.

'Come on, love,' she said softly. 'You'll feel better when you've had something to eat. I'll help you look for it tomorrow.'

She guided him over to the kitchen table.

'You sit down here. You're worn out.'

Barbara pushed a cardboard box over to Fred.

'See if you can find the jam.'

She put the bread in the toaster.

'All this moving house takes it out of us both. Still, I've got a good feeling about this one, Fred. We can really make a fresh start here. Look, I've already planted that little tree your sister gave us.'

I will be strong, Barbara said to herself, and we will be happy here. It's time to bury the past. She looked out of the window again at the Japanese Maple tree standing bravely in its new spot in the garden, safe in the freshly dug earth with the daffodil bulbs she'd planted among its roots.

A memory of other daffodils threatened to sweep her strength away. Painted yellow and white they bloomed on the shining surface of the biscuit tin. She bowed her head, closed her eyes and saw. Sacred pictures placed gently inside the tin: a babe in arms, a golden-haired, muddy-faced boy, a young man in mortarboard and gown, and that same young man with a long-ago version of Fred grinning beside a car, waving a set of L plates. Beneath them other treasures: a dog-eared birth certificate, faded plastic rattle, swimming badges carefully unpicked and wrapped in tissue paper. And, hidden away at the bottom, a charred driving licence folded inside a plastic evidence bag. She willed away the memories of waking, night after night, to the soft click of the tin's lid. Of Fred laying the contents out on the bed, picking over them like the pieces of a puzzle he would never solve.

Barbara looked down at her hands, at the dark soil under her fingernails. Then out of the kitchen window at the little maple tree with precious daffodils hidden at its roots.

Five Minutes to Closing at the Village Shop

I'd left the list at home. There I was standing outside
the village shop, five minutes to closing, no time to get
home and back, and no mobile phone. My mind's a
sieve these days – my mother calls it baby-brain. I call
it sleep deprivation. All I could think of was
chocolate. And all I could remember was the fact that
chocolate was certainly not the thing I'd dashed to the
shop for.

Maybe I'd remember if I looked round the shelves.
I didn't get very far – Valerie, chattiest of all the chatty
volunteers who keep the place running, was behind
the counter.

'Hello, Lucy! How are you? How's the family? Twins over their chickenpox? Baby didn't get it?'

She came bustling over to look in the pram. 'Oh, what a little cutie!'

'Yes. Er no, they're fine now. No he didn't. Thank you. We're all fine.'

'That's good news. At least they'll be back at nursery. Two less under your feet. Come in for a few bits?'

'Yes.'

Shush Valerie, I thought. Shush, shush, shush. I can't think while you're talking to me.

Valerie chatted away. The more she spoke, the less I remembered. My mind kept grasping at chocolate. I picked up a big bar of Green and Blacks and popped it in my basket.

'My favourite!' Valerie licked her lips. 'What a treat! Though I shouldn't really, of course. Did I tell you I've gone back to slimming club? They're so nice there. You should come along one week. Oh, I didn't mean ... Of course you ... When you're ready to lose the baby fat ... Not that ... After all, four children in four years ...'

Valerie's chat tailed off leaving my baby fat and me to waddle around the shop, searching for something to jog our memory. We stopped by the newspapers. Local paper – David said the car was about to be condemned. I added a copy of the Herald, and the latest Marie-Claire (there really was life before children) to my basket. Something from the grocery shelves? Sundried tomatoes – I love those, even if they make the baby's face screw up when he's feeding. Ah ha! If it's urgent, it must be something for the baby.

Eventually, half an hour after closing time (Valerie insisted on hearing a full report of the twins' chickenpox and reciprocated by telling me, at length, about her struggles to find a care home for her elderly mother) I walked home clutching my six items. I'd remembered there were six on the list and had gone for: chocolate, local paper, Marie-Claire, sundried tomatoes, baby wipes and a small pack of nappies. I'd remembered nappies at the last moment, but I hesitated, certain that I'd forgotten something. Was it bread? Was it loo rolls? Oh well, David could always coax our ailing car out to the all-night supermarket.

I could hear the twins fighting even before I put my key in the lock. Their two-year old sister was chanting 'Daddy! Daddy!' which changed to 'Mummy! Mummy!' as soon as she saw me come in.

David looked round the kitchen door, red faced and harassed, a saucepan in one hand, a tea towel in the other.

'You took your time. I was about to send out a search party. Have you got the milk?'

Milk, I thought. Of course.

David was staring at me, then past me into the porch.

'Lucy,' he said. 'Where's the baby?'

Queenie's Last Chance

Nobody could ever have considered Betty Littleton to be an animal lover. As a child, she never felt any desire to hold her friends' hamsters or rabbits. She shunned cuddly bears or other fluffy toys, preferring dolls made of reassuringly rigid plastic. Nor was she ever moved to pet a dog or cat in the street. There was no underlying phobia, simply a complete lack of interest in creatures great or small that continued from childhood, into adolescence, and throughout her adult life. Be they furred, feathered or scaly, she remained indifferent. Which was why Betty's friends were rather more than surprised when, at the age of seventy-two and a quarter, she got herself a dog.

Not just any dog. Betty Littleton's dog was an ungainly blend of wolfhound and giant poodle. On its hind legs, it was much taller than Betty, who stood a petite four feet eleven inches in height. And it was certainly hairier than Betty, who sported a neat little perm that resembled a white knitted hat. In fact, it was a great big bruiser of a dog, the sort you wouldn't want to meet in a dark alley. Which was exactly where Betty and the dog first met.

It was half past nine on a chilly November evening and Betty Littleton was walking home from the Memorial Hall. The Tuesday night sequence dance was one of the highlights of Betty's week, but she was in a sour mood. That very evening, her arch rival, Claudia Coop had helped herself to both Betty's usual seat and her favourite partner, Fred Trimley. Claudia had clung onto Fred for the first half of the evening, even during the rumba, which was Betty's signature dance. She watched the ridiculous spectacle with her friend Audrey and the other wall-flowers. Claudia towered over Fred, his cleanly shaven chin on a level with her more than ample cleavage, while her long, alarmingly auburn hair tickled the end of his nose. When Claudia Coop won the bottle of sherry in the weekly raffle, Betty nearly choked on her mini Bakewell tart and, telling everyone she had a headache, left early. Perhaps she might have mentioned the simmering indignation that had brought the headache on, but that was something Audrey and the other ladies didn't need to know about, so Betty said nothing.

She was just passing the alleyway between the Pound Shop and the Post Office when a gloved hand reached out and grabbed at her bag. Betty screamed, staggered, but didn't fall, thanks to her sensible shoes. The bag, hand, and all that was attached to it disappeared into the darkness of the alley. With a snort of indignation, Betty Littleton gave chase. She didn't need to, she always kept her purse, keys and other valuables safe inside her coat, but that bag contained her best dancing shoes (silver with diamante bows) and Betty felt she'd put up with enough nonsense for one evening.

Despite the lights from the High Street it was very dark in the alley. The far end was lit by a lamppost on Victory Road. But the lamppost suddenly disappeared behind something bulky and thug-shaped. Betty turned to run, but another dark shape crawled out from the shadows, blocking her escape. The second shape growled menacingly. Although not normally given to screaming, Betty Littleton screamed for the second time that evening.

The bulky thug-shaped thing screamed too, dropped the stolen bag, and fled. The growling, shadowy thing brushed past Betty, chasing her assailant out into Victory Road then lolloped back down the alley pausing to scoop up the bag in its jaws. With trembling fingers, Betty turned on the little torch she always carried on dark evenings and the growling, lolloping, shadowy mass transformed into the biggest, scruffiest dog she had ever seen.

The dog looked at Betty.

Betty looked at the dog.

'Sit' she said sharply. And the dog sat.

At that moment, a middle-aged man arrived in the alleyway. He was carrying a lead. 'Queenie!' he puffed. 'There you are. Here, girl!'

The dog stayed put.

'I'm sorry if she frightened you,' the man said to Betty. 'Queenie wouldn't hurt a fly, but she's so disobedient. Always running off. We're the fourth family she's been placed with, and it's just not working. Oh, Queenie,' he added sadly, 'you're going to have to go back and you know what that means … We were your last chance.'

Queenie looked at Betty. Betty looked right back, drawing herself up to her full four feet and eleven inches.

'My bag, please.' she said. The dog gently placed the bag at her feet. Still looking Queenie in the eye, Betty Littleton said, 'I might be in the market for a dog, myself.'

The warden at the Pet Rescue Centre took some persuading. Naturally, she was concerned that Betty (four feet eleven inches tall, slight of build, seventy-two-and-a-quarter years old) would never be able to handle a dog of Queenie's size and temperament. But she was amazed by Betty's authority over the animal.

'You must have a lot of experience with dogs,' the warden remarked.

Betty could have mentioned that she had no experience at all. But that was something the warden didn't need to know, so she said nothing.

The warden was so relieved to be rid of Queenie that she made only a cursory follow up visit, and was happy to report that the arrangement appeared to suit both Betty and the dog. Those who knew her well, however, were more than surprised.

'Well, I am amazed!' said Audrey, understating the obvious.

'I'm Queenie's last chance,' Betty told them, eyes locked with the dog's. 'And she's company for me. I've been rather lonely since Clive passed on. Besides,' she added, 'there's so much crime on the streets these days. I feel much safer now I've got Queenie with me.'

After that, everywhere Betty went the dog went too. Even to the Tuesday evening sequence dance, where Queenie sat with all the other ladies and kept a guard on Betty's favourite chair. Fred came over to join them.

'We're only allowed budgies at the flats,' he said, scratching Queenie behind her ears. 'It's a real shame 'cos I always had a dog when I was younger.'

'I remember you saying,' Betty replied. 'How about you come over for lunch tomorrow? Then we could take Queenie out for a walk in the afternoon.'

'Grand idea,' said Fred. 'Fancy a rumba?'

Betty took his hand. 'No Claudia this evening?'

'Oh, she was here earlier, sneezing and coughing all over the place. She had to go home.'

Perhaps Betty Littleton might have mentioned that Audrey had told her about Claudia Coop's allergy to dog hair. But that was something Fred didn't need to know, so she said nothing.

eleven weeks and five days

She's sitting in the car and she's silent – absolutely, atypically silent. He's driving (all profile and dark glasses) and she's sitting and thinking and thinking. And trying not to think at all. 'Crazy Frog' is on the radio, it's always on the radio. The only CD in the car is 'The Wheels on the Bus', but there's nobody in the back to sing along because Maisie is safe at a friend's house, playing with the cats. She reaches a finger to the dashboard and turns off the noise.

They pass the Bournville factory. The thought of chocolate makes her nauseous. Her mouth is dry, her hands are sweating. Her head is so light her mind might float away. Perhaps they won't be able to find the place. Perhaps there won't be room in the car park.

Perhaps, her heart jumps at the thought, they'll be late and miss the appointment. Or perhaps they've got the wrong day. Maybe this isn't really happening at all.

He takes a ticket from the machine at the barrier and parks the car. She gets out slowly. Tucks her hair behind her ears. It needs highlighting, it needs a decent cut. Her stretchy trousers feel tight; this time around she's already lost her waist. But she has mascara and lipstick for courage, and a bag over her shoulder with spare knickers and pads, and The Book. He takes her hand and they walk through the car park together, step by step by step.

Birmingham Women's Hospital. They stand in front of a big sign with a long list of departments. She can't focus to read, but he can: 'Department of Fetal Medicine and Cytogenics'. They walk briskly now, following the arrows. There's a fork in the corridors – what if they took a wrong turning? What if they just stopped walking right here? She could stop this. She could say no. Her throat is too dry to speak. Her cheeks are wet and hot, her head heavy now. At least her mind is staying put. He is half a pace ahead, still holding her hand. He passes her a tissue although he can't see her tears.

She has had five miscarriages and one daughter – Maisie, their two-year old miracle, perfect and precious. She is forty-five, too old for this. She should count her blessings, not push her luck. Above all, she has no business risking her family's happiness, her daughter's future.

The Book has the statistics:

Mother's age at delivery	Risk of chromosome abnormality at full term
40	1:100
42	1:55
45	1:15

Maisie was one of the blessed 54:55. But that 1:15 would turn their lives inside out. She's seen her friend's boy. She understands what Down's syndrome could mean. With parents already deep into middle-age, a life sentence for Maisie as her sibling's carer. And so they agreed, he and she agreed, no risk would be small enough. As though anything less than normal might infect them all.

He leads her to a desk and she hands over a slip of paper, damp with sweat from her hand. The receptionist has a brisk lip-sticked smile. He talks, perhaps she does too. They go to some seats behind a pink and lilac screen. A screen that hides them from the corridor. That hides the corridor's tactless procession of ordinary lives from them. They hold hands.

'Are you still feeling sick? Do you want a wine gum?'

She shakes her head and he looks at his watch.

'Not long now. Better finish this.'

He hands her a bottle of water and she drains the last few mouthfuls, wondering how her bladder will hold them.

A nurse comes and sits beside her. She is round and middle-aged and doesn't smile too much.

'I'm so sorry, we're running late. Can I get you anything?'

No.

'A drink of water?'

God No.

'It shouldn't be more than twenty minutes.'

She thinks of other waiting rooms, sitting amongst the women with swollen bellies. Waiting to hear that her five babies were definitely dead. She puts a hand on her belly now. This baby is alive.

She tries to smile at the nurse: to be civilised, grown-up, in control. Twenty more minutes. They could just go home.

Their hands are hot so she untangles her fingers. It's June. Too hot to sit in an airless corridor, hidden behind a curtain, watching the sky through a window high above them. Too hot to hang on to sweaty flesh, but she needs his touch. So they sit with the length of their thighs touching, backsides cheek by cheek on the slippery plastic seats. Her legs are sticky in the stretchy trousers. Her head is light, her lips bitten to raw, salty meat. Her eyes are wet, flitting, looking for somewhere to land, to ground herself. She sees the notice board, the leaflets, the pictures of babies, the telephone numbers of the support groups. She picks up her handbag and takes out The Book, opens it at one of the folded down pages:

'Chorionic villus sampling (CVS)
Detects similar abnormalities to amniocentesis, but is performed earlier in pregnancy.
In the best hands the risk of miscarriage as a result of the test is 1-3 percent'

Once more she searches between the facts for some small certainty that all will be well. Recalculates the figures she's worked so many times before. 1 to 3 percent risk of miscarriage - say 2:100, that's 1:50. Versus 1:15 risk of Down's. 50 versus 15. Does that make it 10 to 3 that she's doing the right thing? She looks at him. He is silent, looking up at the window. They've talked this over so many times there is nothing left unsaid. It always comes down to the numbers for him. For her it will always come down to feelings.

Twenty minutes behave strangely. Fifteen drag their feet, then five speed up to a sprint. Another twenty come unannounced, some crawling, some running. When she is sure she must wet herself or burst, at last, the nurse hurries back.

'I'm so sorry you've had to wait. You can come through now. I'll explain the procedure to you, then I need you to sign a form.'

'Can my husband come with me? I want him to be with me.' She has found her voice again. Perhaps he talks too.

'The baby and placenta are located by ultrasound scan; tissue is removed from the edge of the placenta, through the abdomen...and cultured or examined directly.'

The room smells ruthlessly clean, but it is darkened and calm. They are all dressed in green: two doctors, another nurse who's taller and younger, and her nurse, the middle-aged one who brought her in. She takes off her trousers, climbs onto the bed and rolls her knickers down to her pubic hair. They are all talking quietly and kindly. The young doctor with the glasses will put a needle in her belly, while the one with the beard watches it all on the screen. The tall nurse will assist. The other nurse will hold her hand.

'Can I have a tissue, darling?'

He takes out a little packet, hands her a clean tissue. She holds it in her right hand while the nurse holds her left. Tears trickle unchecked into her ears. Her face is hot, her ears and hair are wet. From time to time she glances quickly at her baby on the screen, but she doesn't want to watch. He watches for them both.

Her belly is anaesthetised. The needle feels strange, unwelcome, like someone scratching inside. That's what the doctor is doing, scraping up some cells to test. So that she'll know if her baby has to die. The test is a taster of the guilt: a 2:100 risk to their baby's life weighed up against the 1:15 risk to their cosy family. A taster of guilt to prepare her in case there is worse guilt to come.

And then it's done. She's survived this far. She's cried, but she hasn't disgraced herself, she hasn't broken down. They go into another room and a nurse brings tea. She thinks about toast – baby things, (births and D&Cs) are always followed by toast. Instead there is another piece of paper. Things to look out for, what's normal after the procedure and what could be a sign of that 2:100 miscarriage.

It is her turn to talk. 'Thank you, you've been very kind.'

'You should hear in ten to fourteen days - we try to call between six and seven in the evening. Will there be someone at home with you at that time?'

They nod. He holds her hand and they walk back to the car. Her legs are cold, light and wobbly, her head is hot and heavy, her face wet with tears that won't stop. It's June, it's sunny and warm, but she's shivering.

A little later, after the risk of miscarriage is past but before she's had the phone call, someone asks: 'Did it hurt?' She thinks about it. On her belly there is a bruise the size of the doctor's fist. But no, it didn't hurt, although something is still scratching away inside her. She thinks it might be scratching at her soul.

Women in Shorts

She asked for Bradley's favourite table, the one looking down onto the beach with a view of the esplanade and the town beyond, gleaming and white in the Mediterranean sun.

The café stood on a small promontory of rock, jutting out into the sea and, from her seat, she could see the sand just a few metres below, yellow-white with a small, roughly circular patch of grey; a pale mound not far from the shoreline. Her own footprints were already beginning to fade – the tide came in so quickly at this end of the bay.

'Senora?'

He was the same waiter who had served them last year, and the year before, every year that she could remember. Each time they had returned to an effusive welcome, but the waiter didn't seem to recognise her without Bradley walking a pace or two ahead. And she didn't have enough Spanish to explain the situation.

She ordered coffee and a pastry. It was strange, confusing almost, without Bradley there to choose for her, so she ordered what they always had. Then, as the waiter turned away, she called him back.

'And a brandy. I'd like a brandy please. Por favor.'

She wished she could speak Spanish. Bradley always spoke Spanish in the shops and cafes and she felt exposed to be here alone.

But the waiter just smiled. 'Si, Senora. I will bring it.'

It was ridiculously early for brandy, of course, but it was too late to change her mind – the waiter had already gone.

She looked down at the sand. The tide had reached the patch of grey, already the edges had begun to blur. She blinked and reached into her bag for a tissue, then realised she didn't need it after all, and looked away towards the promenade and the road into town.

It was a colourful scene. Holiday makers off on excursions or for a day on the beach. A carnival of tropical prints, brightly coloured hats and exposed skin in every shade of beige, brown and pink. Bradley would have had a few comments to make about the flesh on display, how people dressed when they came to these places, when there was no risk of bumping into the people they saw every day back in Woking or Slough. Even when he was wearing sunglasses she could sense the disapproval in his eyes at each middle-aged woman displaying her pudgy or wrinkled knees to the world at large.

'What do they think they look like? It's enough to put a man off his lunch,' Bradley would mutter. 'Thank God you have the sense to cover up.'

She perceived a different reaction whenever a younger, lither, longer-legged woman passed by. Even though his eyes were hidden behind the shades, she knew where Bradley was looking. And every now and then she'd hear a low whistle escaping from his lips, without him even noticing it had happened.

Buttoned up, covered up, she envied the women in shorts. Not just the lovely young creatures Bradley admired. She envied them all: their holiday smiles, their lack of concern about how their lower limbs, or any other part of them, looked in their holiday clothes. Most of all, she envied the feeling of the sea air on the backs of their knees when all she could feel was the sticky dampness of her sensible cotton trousers.

Once, was it really more than twenty years ago, the second or third time they'd come to the resort, she'd ventured to suggest: 'I think I might get a pair of shorts this holiday. Not the really short ones, of course, something more discreet.'

'Hm?' Bradley barely looked up from his magazine.

'Shorts, dear. I think I'll get myself some shorts for our holiday.'

The laugh was spontaneous, mocking, and final.

'You? Shorts? With your fat little legs? I don't think so.'

She drank the brandy first then, feeling a little lightheaded, sipped her coffee as she picked the pastry to crumbs – Bradley would have had something to say about that too. She sighed. How tiring to be married to a man who, every year, seemed a little more disappointed with his choice of wife. And how easy it had been to be distracted from so many disappointments of her own.

She would have liked to holiday further afield, but why waste money when they had the timeshare. She had always loved bright colours, but Bradley preferred her in classic, neutral shades. Her own little car would have been nice, but so unnecessary when they could do a supermarket shop together on a Saturday. As for children … She reached for another tissue.

'Senora?'

The waiter was back. 'The pastry was not good, Senora?'

'No. No, it's fine, very nice. It's me. I just … Could I have the bill?'

'Of course,' he paused. 'Senor Bradley is not with you today?'

She looked down at the beach. The tide was already half way up the sand. The patch of grey had been washed away beneath the water.

'No. Not anymore.'

Over on the promenade, a group of women posed for a seaside snap, their smiles wide and carefree, their legs all lengths and widths and shades of pink and brown. How tragic, she thought, that her own fat little legs had been too short and slow to fetch help when Bradley's coronary struck.

She paid the waiter for the first and final time, adding a generous tip.

'Gracias, Senora Bradley,' he said as she rose to leave.

'Mary,' she said firmly. 'My name is Mary.'

'Then, Senora Mary, I would like to say that you are looking very lovely in your pretty outfit. It is perfect for such a beautiful day.'

Mary looked down at her clothes, the sunshine-yellow blouse and sky-blue shorts, her legs below self-tanned to an attractive mid-bronze.

'Thank you,' she replied. 'Yes, it is.'

Picture Perfect

It was early evening when the college porter knocked. Cressida, who had just finished tidying her desk, dropped a crumpled tissue into the wastepaper basket before she answered the door. She took the parcel from his outstretched hand with thanks and a gracious smile. The clock beside her bed showed seven forty-three. Seventeen minutes before the Social was due to start – just enough time to see what was inside.

Beneath the layers of packaging, there was a heavy, flat oblong, about thirty by forty centimetres, in gold embossed wrapping with a co-ordinating bow. Cressida looked at it in silence. Then she carefully peeled off the sticky tape, unfolding several sheets of paper to reveal a gift box containing a photograph album bound in creamy gold leather, with a little card which read, as she knew it would:

PICTURE PERFECT

To Our Golden Girl,
with love from
Mummy and Daddy
xxxx
We know you will make us proud

Cressida opened the album and turned the pages, slowly and carefully, on a catalogue of achievements, an impressive showcase of the pictures and mementoes on permanent display in her parents' drawing room. Images of their golden girl, at varying ages and heights, clutching trophies for ballet, or horse-riding, or tennis. Prizes and certificates for maths challenges, spelling bees, and sundry other competitions. Photographs of her receiving awards at speech days and sports days. And, of course, a serene and smiling Cressida holding the letter confirming her place at Cambridge.

The last page was blank, reserved for one final image. Cressida pictured a family group: her in the centre in mortarboard and gown, her parents on either side in smart new clothes. A celebration of her Cambridge degree, which would, as everybody predicted, be both first class and with distinction.

Such was the anticipated payback for all those years dining on sandwiches from plastic tubs as Cressida's mother drove her to tutors, or ballet classes, or choir practice. Of pony club and the tennis club. Holidays in Classical Greece and Rome – even a trek along the Great Wall of China to consolidate her Mandarin.

Each opportunity identified, scheduled, and paid for. Every investment, her parents constantly reassured her, was well worth the money. No sacrifice could be too great in the bid to maximise their daughter's exceptional potential.

Cressida ran her finger over the album's cover feeling for scratches or defects – there were none. It was made from a single piece of perfect leather, embossed with her name and date of birth in a deeper shade of gold. The perfect setting to capture the culmination of her parents' ambitions. A solid reminder of all she was expected to achieve. She placed it carefully back in the gift box and put it on the shelf beside her bed, next to the clock that was already set to wake her at five the next morning; that woke her at five every morning.

The clock showed eight-thirteen. Cressida was already late and she hated to be late. She took a deep breath, then another, letting each breath out very slowly as she checked her appearance in the full-length mirror on her closet door. Her top was understated but pretty, her jeans expensively distressed, her hair glossy, pale and golden as the photograph album, with a perfect plait on one side. Her makeup was subtle and her smile, when she smiled, looked natural and welcoming – confident yet without arrogance.

She smoothed out the discarded wrapping paper, folding it carefully then folding it again, sharpening each crease with the back of her thumb nail, repeating the action until she was satisfied. Then she positioned it in the top of the wastepaper basket over a mess of crushed and bloodstained tissues.

Cressida pulled on a cardigan with fashionably overlong sleeves that hid the freshly scored lines on her forearms. She checked the time again, screwed her hands into tight little fists, and set off to show her fellow Freshers just what perfection looked like in the flesh.

Monty and Jules

Act 1

Monty usually gave the Tuesday afternoon tea dance a wide berth. But his son and daughter-in-law had the decorators in at the pub, poncing up the place. Monty felt unsettled, and unwanted. And old. They were stripping the life (his life) out of the bar, replacing it with stylishly uncomfortable sofas and expensive lights made from recycled beer bottles that gave off a feeble glow. Next, it would be piddly little portions of monkfish served up on slates with a splat of pea puree – he'd seen her flicking through those foodie magazines. Besides, they were both still ranting because the council had refused planning permission for their conservatory function room as 'not in keeping with the rural character of the village'. As usual they held one person responsible: Councillor Geraldine Capp, known locally as the CBloodyC.

'Funny there was no objection to that tacky little cottage at the bottom of her garden,' his daughter-in-law snorted. 'All that fretwork and gables and that sodding balcony overlooking my frontage – and I know for a fact she took a bung from the builders on that new development at Verona Crescent.'

Monty was desperate to get out for a bit. And, since the allotments (and, consequently, his private stash of bottled beer) were under water after the recent rain, he let his mate Ben drag him along to the tea dance in the village hall. Although Monty knew he'd have to tread carefully. Rose was on refreshments – and they had history.

Soon as he walked in, Monty saw the new girl sitting on the edge of the stage, swinging her legs in time to the music. A spotlight of sunshine lit her hair like a halo of cropped silver. The other women, who looked like they'd crocheted old grey wool on top of their heads, had her surrounded as they jostled to pitch their favourite clubs and causes. Monty, timing his swoop on the refreshments table for when Rose was busy in the kitchen, grabbed a cuppa and a fistful of custard creams, then found himself a seat with a view.

The new girl was a few years younger than him (seventy at the most), a few inches shorter, and a good a few stone lighter. She noticed him staring and blushed like a teenager. Monty grinned back, then realised he was blushing too. As the couples paired up for the next dance, he made his move.

'Monty.' He stuck out a warm, brawny palm.

'Jules.'

Her fingers were long and cool and he was inspired to raise them to his lips.

'Shall we?'

It was years since he'd taken to the floor, but Monty was relieved to find his feet still remembered a passable foxtrot. Jules was delightfully light on her feet, and in his arms, and it took him right back.

He ventured a little small talk. 'Not just passing through, I hope.'

'No,' she smiled. 'I've just moved into the village. To be closer to my daughter.'

'The new houses at Verona Crescent?'

Jules nodded. 'Near there.'

'Used to be an orchard – I went scrumping there when we were lads. My son and his wife organised a petition to stop the build, but it got pushed through in the end. They were at loggerheads with the CBloodyC for over a year.'

'See-bloody-what?'

'Oh, just local stuff. They look nice, those houses. Rather fancy one myself.'

'Where do you live?'

'Over the pub – The Montague Arms.'

'Ah, Monty as in Montague?'

'Yeah. And no. That Montague was a seventeenth century nobleman. I'm Montague Tanner – my mother's idea to tie the family in with the pub. She was a great believer in the importance of a name.'

Monty found his feet also remembered the rumba. He even found the energy for the tango. As he dipped Jules for the third time, she smiled a flirty little smile. What a woman! thought Monty. She could teach those poncy new light fittings at the pub a thing or two about burning brightly.

When the dancing was over, he offered to walk her home. As they passed The Montague Arms, Jules looked up at the sign swinging outside.

'So, are you the landlord?'

'Used to be. And my dad before me. Had some high old times when the missus was alive. My son's taken over the running now. Him and his wife.' Monty pulled a face.

Jules gave his hand a squeeze. 'Children, eh? My daughter's even more of a tyrant than her dad was!'

'Why'd you move here then?'

'I've had a bit of heart trouble over the past couple of years. Oh, just a flutter – nothing to get worked up about. My daughter says it's more convenient to have me close by. But I'm still an independent woman – what I get up to in the privacy of my own home is my own business.'

She smiled her mischievous smile again and Monty felt a little flutter of his own.

Jules excused herself, saying she needed to put her feet up after all that dancing. Monty lingered outside the pub, a twinkle in his eye and a whistle on his lips. He'd call round tomorrow – with flowers from the allotment, if any had survived the rain. And then he'd ask her out to lunch. In the meantime, he was gasping for a pint after all that tea, and here was Ben, right on cue.

'You're living dangerously, Monty Tanner!'

Monty stopped whistling. 'What d'you mean?'

'Your new girlfriend – didn't she tell you who her daughter is? Only Councillor Geraldine Bloody Capp!'

Across the pub car park, away over a tall garden wall, Monty could see a little gabled cottage and his lady love waving from the balcony.

Act 2

Jules made friends with the nurse who lived next door and asked if she could walk her spaniel in the mornings; with four children to get ready for school, the nurse was delighted. Monty's son was amazed when his dad started dragging the pub's elderly labrador out at the crack of dawn, but Monty told him the GP insisted he lose twenty pounds and taking up dog walking was less traumatic than giving up beer.

Every day, at six-thirty am, their paths crossed, accidentally, and they strolled together along the track that led up the hill and over the fields in a three-mile loop. Once out of sight, they held hands. Some mornings, they came across the vicar and his poodles, but the man of God was also the soul of discretion. All the same, Jules feared it was only a matter of time before the gossip reached their families and the dog doo-doo hit the fan.

The evening after the tea dance, Jules had suggested a meal at The Montague Arms. Councillor Geraldine Capp wasted neither time nor breath in setting her mother straight.

'Those Tanners! Three generations of land-lording and they think they're local gentry. Did I tell you they tried to sabotage the Verona Crescent development? They even objected to your lovely chalet!' She waved her arm around Jules' tiny kitchen-diner. 'And such vulgar pretensions – conservatory function room indeed. Well I soon put a stop to that! No Capp will ever set foot in The Montague Arms! As Shakespeare would put it: A sprig of limp parsley doth not a gastro-pub make.'

That's Lovelace, not Shakespeare. She's even misquoting the wrong poet, Jules thought, reminded of her dead husband. Geraldine hadn't just inherited her father's profile, but some very unattractive aspects of his personality. Just as it had seemed pragmatic to keep her own counsel on so many subjects over forty years of marriage, Jules kept the details of her star-crossed romance locked in her own bosom.

There was no need to mention her new dog-walking routine – Geraldine was never awake before eight in the morning. Nor the tea dance – Geraldine was always at the council offices on a Tuesday afternoon. And Jules certainly didn't mention the nights Monty had crept through Councillor Capp's moonlit garden, stealing away again before the sunrise.

'It's not that we're doing anything wrong,' she told Monty as they sat in bed swigging beer from the bottle. 'But she'd make such a terrible fuss.'

Monty agreed. 'They'd kick-off at the pub too.'

'So we'll just keep things as they are?'

Monty nodded, drained his beer and snuggled up for another cuddle.

Perhaps it was Monty's old flame, Rose, who dropped them in it. It definitely wasn't the vicar, nor his poodles. Nor was it the nurse next door – she thought

'Good luck to them!' But it was the nurse who heard the row from over the fence as Councillor Capp confronted her mother about the outrageous gossip that was the talk of the village shop, the WI, and the local hairdresser's. And it was the nurse who came running when she heard the Councillor's screams and found Jules crumpled in a deck chair, breathing raggedly and clutching at her heart.

The vicar saw the ambulance, blue light flashing, and hurried to The Montague Arms.

'He's down the allotments with Ben,' Monty's son snorted. 'Hiding.'

'You can tell the old fool from me not to bother coming back,' the daughter-in-law added with a scowl. 'Bloody traitor's been dipping his wick in the CBloodyC's gene pool!'

Ben gave Monty a lift to the hospital where the vicar met him and took him up to Intensive Care. But, not being family, they weren't allowed in. And Councillor Capp wouldn't talk to them.

Monty didn't go back to the pub. He lay low at the allotment, locking himself in the shed when Ben or the vicar came looking for him. After a couple of days, he'd exhausted his stash of beer and decided to walk the three mile loop up the hill and across the fields – in memory of the mornings he'd shared with Jules. But Monty had developed a bad cough from sleeping in the damp shed and he barely made it to the edge of the village before he had to lie down by the side of the road. Which was where the nurse found him as she drove home from the hospital.

There were so many flowers: from Ben, the vicar, the nurse. A lovely arrangement from the ladies at the tea dance.

'How sad that something so beautiful should last so short a while,' the nurse sighed, stooping to read the card on a splendid display of white roses and lilies.

'Hm?' Jules was watching Monty struggle with two enormous suitcases. 'Oh, take whichever you want. They'll only be dead by the time we get back.'

'What in the name of ... What have you got in here, woman?' Monty set the cases down with a thump.

'We'll be away for a month. I need lots of lovely clothes for all that dining and dancing.' Jules giggled and smiled her flirty smile.

The nurse laughed. 'Are you sure you're both up to it?'

'Oh yes. The doctors said a cruise would be just the thing. Then, when we get back, our lovely new house in Verona Crescent should be ready.' Jules sighed, 'I can't wait to get shot of this pokey place – and that dreadful view of the pub car park!'

'Has Councillor Capp come around yet?'

'Nope,' said Monty. 'And we're still barred from the Montague Arms.'

'Never mind,' said Jules. 'We really shouldn't be living in our families' pockets. It's not as if we're teenagers anymore.'

Natural Talent

I've told Sadie not to worry because Everything Will be All Right on the Night. Mummy says that's what people say in the theatre although, actually, we're performing in the afternoon, not at night. I crossed my fingers behind my back when I said it, but it wasn't really a lie, it was what Mummy calls Wishful Thinking. Besides, Sadie is my fourth best friend and I was being kind.

We're doing a dance, Sadie and I. In the 'Step Up to Stardom Show'. Mummy entered us in the 7 Years and Under category. We've got bunches of ribbons in all colours of the rainbow and we're dancing to 'Any Dream Will Do'. Mummy sewed the ribbons onto our dresses because Sadie's mummy isn't very good at sewing. And we've had to do lots of rehearsing because if we do really well in the Local competition, we go through to the Regionals. Then it's just one more step to the Final!

Mummy says I have what you call Natural Talent. The problem is Sadie. She's rubbish at dancing. She gets all nervous and forgets the steps. Usually she forgets to wave her ribbons. Sometimes she forgets to dance at all. And I have to do all the singing, because Sadie's only got a tiny little voice and she can't remember the words. It isn't really her fault, she's a summer baby. She isn't even six yet. I'm going to be seven on the first of September. So, at school I have to look after Sadie and tell her what to do.

Secretly, Mummy and I are a bit worried. It's a shame I couldn't do the dance with Bella, she's my very best friend, but she won't be back from Cornwall. And Jess doesn't like dancing. And Amelia's mummy has fallen out with my mummy. So, Sadie's the best we can do.

But we've got a plan. I'm going to make sure I dance right in front of Sadie and then people won't notice so much when she messes it up. And because I'm taller than her (well I am nearly a whole year older) then they'll hardly have to see Sadie at all.

It's nearly time to go on. There's a man with a clipboard and he says we're on next. Mummy says I better not say Break a Leg like they do in the theatre or Sadie might think she's supposed to fall off the stage!

*　　　*　　　*

Well that was One Major Balls Up. That's what Daddy would say. Mummy says it sometimes too if something goes very, very wrong. When it was our turn, Sadie cried and said she didn't want to go on, but all of us (Mummy, me, even Sadie's mummy) said she had to. Only now I wish she hadn't.

When the music started, Sadie just stood there staring. Well that was all right, I started dancing and it sounds better when she doesn't sing. I waved my ribbons and I was in perfect time and projecting my voice like Mummy told me to. All Sadie had to do was not get in the way.

I could see our mummies in the audience. My mummy had her bright smile on and was clapping her hands to keep time. Sadie's mummy was pulling faces and making little circles with her hands, like she was holding ribbons too. I didn't let her put me off, even though it was rather distracting. But then, all of a sudden, Sadie started jumping about over the place and waving her ribbons in the air. It was like she was dancing to a completely different song. It was awful. Sadie skipped and hopped. Round and round. Right at the front of the stage. I had to go and dance in the wrong place so the audience could see me, but there wasn't enough room and we kept bumping into each other. Then Sadie started singing, only she just sang 'La La La' because she couldn't remember the words. And she was really loud so I had to sing louder and louder too. I was nearly shouting by the time we finished.

Everybody laughed at us, and I wanted to cry. But, like Mummy says, The Show Must Go On. So I had to bite my lip and do a curtsey and pretend everything really was all right on the night

Now lots of people are standing up and clapping. But Mummy isn't clapping. She looks really cross — she's just standing there like she's too cross to move. Sadie's mummy is pushing her way through the crowd. She must be coming to tell Sadie off and make her say sorry for spoiling our dance.

But why is Sadie's mummy talking to the man with the clipboard? And she's smiling all over her face and hugging Sadie and kissing the top of her head.

'Oh yes!' she's saying, and her voice is all giggly and so loud she's almost shouting. 'Sadie is amazing! Of course, the older girl does a creditable job as her straight-guy. But my daughter has what you'd call Natural Talent.'

Ada's Journey

Seven o'clock

This man's just been on the wireless. Rung up to say everybody seems to be 'on a journey' these days and he was feeling left out. I only put it on for some company. I've been feeling a bit low, what with all this snow we've been having and my arthritis has been that bad this last week. January's a dreary old month, isn't it? So I put on Radio Two over breakfast, but I'm not mad keen on the new chap. I preferred Wogan.

As it happens, I'm going on a journey myself today and never mind the snow. Only Tescos, mind, but still that's something, isn't it. Yesterday afternoon, I was looking out the window at little Alfie playing in the snow – isn't it strange all these kiddies with old folk's names. My granddad was called Alfred. Anyway,

Alfie's mum come over and asked was I OK? She's a kind girl, even if she has got an earring in her nose.

'I'm running a bit low,' I told her. 'Only I can't risk the bus with all this ice. And the cold takes my breath away.'

So they're taking me in the car. And for a bite of lunch in the café.

I'd better get on with my chores so I can be ready when they come. It'll be good to get out – I've been stuck inside over a week. Long as I take my puffer with me, I should be all right.

Eight o'clock

They're still on about journeys. This woman rang in to say she was on a journey to find herself. Well I laughed out loud. 'Try a mirror, love,' I wanted to tell her. 'You'll be the one with the dopey look on her face and too much time on her hands!'

I should have such problems. This place doesn't keep itself clean. I might be over ninety, but every day I'm up with the lark, washed and dressed, bit of breakfast then on with my chores. Doesn't take long now I'm in the bungalow. Of course, I do miss the old house, but our Michael insisted. Said he wanted me where he could keep an eye.

Still, there's plenty to be grateful for. And it doesn't do to waste time moping. Some people spend their days just looking for misery – I get my duster out instead. This morning I'm having a good go at the front room. Started with Mother's copper kettle – oh,

I used to hate the hours I spent shining that blessed thing, but these days it's like an old friend.

'More like old junk' our Michael says.

'That old junk reminds me where I came from,' I tell him. 'And just how far I've come.'

When I met my Walter, I used to drop my 'h's all over the place and I couldn't even find my 'p's and 'q's. Palace Dance Hall, it was. Cardiff 1942. I had a patched-up, second-hand dress and Mother's shoes stuffed with newspaper to make them fit. Walter was smart as paint in his RAF uniform – cut-glass accent to boot. He could have had his pick, but he only had eyes for me – never mind what his family had to say.

'You're lucky to have had him,' I always say to our Michael. 'Your father was such a good man. I never even knew mine, he died before I was born.'

And before Mother had the chance to get him to the alter. She had a struggle to keep a roof over our heads and food in our tummies – there's things I'd be ashamed to tell you, things I never even told Walter. So, when I polish that kettle, I think about Mother and how far I've come from that damp little terrace down by the docks.

Next, I do the photo frames on the mantle-piece. There's a bitter sweet job, all those dear souls moved on now, somewhere in this world or the next. I stop and say hello to each one: Mother; my little brother Ike who took his family out to Australia and never came back; Michael and his kiddies, and their kiddies too. And Walter, of course. I always find time for a little kiss for my Walter.

I didn't get round to the hoovering this morning, good thing it doesn't show too bad on a patterned carpet. I'm just finding it hard to catch my breath.

It's snowing again. I wonder will Alfie's mum want to drive if it's snowing?

Nine o'clock
Postie's just delivered a card from Florida – Michael's eldest on holiday with her kiddies. Folk think nothing of distance nowadays. Florida's just like Barry Island to them.

Mother used to take us to Barry on the train. Oh, she loved the sea. And our Ike did. I'll never forget the first time he went on the sand – running in and out of the waves he was, laughing and laughing. That's why he moved out to Australia – for the ocean. Then he spends the rest of his days telling everyone it's not a patch on Barry Island.

Walter and I went out to see him. There's a snap on the mantelpiece of us all in front of the new Opera House in Sydney. 1975. Took us three days just to get there. All that sitting on aeroplanes – I thought I'd never get my sling-backs on again. And then when you get there you've only got to get home again. But my Walter loved travelling.

'Ada,' he'd say, 'it's such a treat to look down at the beautiful cities of the world knowing you don't have to drop bombs on them.'

ADA'S JOURNEY

He had such plans for his retirement – a journey right round the world. I wasn't mad keen, but I did want to see the Taj Mahal. Mother had a tea caddy with it on where she used to keep the pennies.

Our Michael's always on and off planes. All over Europe, and America too. All airports and board rooms, he says – no time for postcards. I've hardly seen him since I moved here. And that wife of his won't set foot – which is fine by me. I've never seen eye-to-eye with that one. It's no surprise to me our Michael's strayed.

He's abroad again at the moment, Michael and his new girl, Annie. She's from California.

'We need the sun, Mother,' he told me. 'A break from this lousy British weather.'

And who can blame him for that? Money's a bit tight, though – what with the divorce and Annie's baby on the way. And a wedding to plan.

'Don't you worry about the money,' I told Michael. 'There's plenty left over from my old house. Just you make sure and send me a postcard.'

It's probably in the post.

'Fly Me to the Moon'. That's what's on the wireless now. They've been at it all morning with the journeys: 'Long and Winding Road', 'Up, Up and Away in My Beautiful Balloon'. I've been listening out for Walter's favourite, 'Come Fly with Me'. Got my hanky ready.

I dreamed about him again last night.

'Come on, Ada,' he said. 'Come fly with me.'

Oh, but I wanted to go.

Ten o'clock

Now it might be a little bit pokey, but there's one thing this bungalow has got and that's plenty of wardrobes. And all of them chock-a-block with beautiful clothes I never even wear nowadays. I used to love buying clothes. We never had anything new when I was growing up. Every scrap had been worn before – including my unmentionables.

Once I had a bit of cash I'd always spend it on new clothes. First present my Walter ever bought me was a hat – dove grey, with white silk roses and a little net veil. Mother cried when she saw it. Then she told me to watch out what he wanted in return. Well, it was wartime, see. She must have known what we were up to – same as every other couple who didn't know if they'd be dead by the end of the week. But we were careful, and I was luckier than she'd been.

Walter loved to see me well turned out. He was always buying me nice clothes: evening dresses, day dresses, smart little suits. There's some lovely outfits I bought for our trip round the world. Be a shame not to give one of them an airing even if it is just Tescos. Here's a white turtle neck and a lovely pair of black slacks – bit big on the waist these days, but they'll be fine with a belt. And these boots Walter bought me the winter before he died. 1982 – that was a cold one, the thermometer in the back garden touched minus twenty.

It's a shame I can't wear my fur coat, but these days they chuck paint at you for so much as a cony hat. The cashmere will have to do. Then I must put my face on, I haven't been out of the house without makeup since I was sixteen. Always tasteful mind, I'd never have caught Walter's eye if I'd gone round looking like a trollop. Mother wore lipstick every day of her life. When she died I bought her a new one – expensive, for her to look her best on that final journey. She might have worn herself out providing for Ike and me, but Mother always scrubbed up well and I still try to do her proud. Even now I always wear foundation, and a bit of lippy brightens up a winter face.

Now for the finishing touch – a very special brooch. Ruby red to match my lips.

Eleven o'clock
Alfie's mum is going to do my shopping for me. I've given her a bit extra for a treat in the cafe. When I stepped outside the front door it was that cold I just couldn't catch my breath.

She wanted to call the doctor.

'I'll be all right,' I told her. 'I've just overdone it a bit this morning.'

So, she fetched my puffer, and we all had a rich tea biscuit and a cuppa. In the old days, I'd have made Welsh cakes, but I can't get on with the oven in this bungalow. I do miss my old kitchen. And my old neighbours. Well, we'd known each other fifty years.

'Half of them are already dead, Mother,' our Michael says. 'And the others are half dead already.'

Alfie's mum is such a kind girl. She got me settled in my chair and hung up my coat. She noticed my brooch and I told her Walter gave it me for our fortieth anniversary.

'We only had a little registry office wedding,' I told her. 'Just Walter and me, my brother Ike and Mother in a new hat. Walter's family said we wouldn't last the year. But we did – we lasted forty.'

Exactly forty years. It was just after Walter retired. He signed the business over to Michael and off we went. First stop on our round the world trip was India. All the heat and the bustle. And the blessed cool and calm of the best hotel in Agra. We were having our dinner in this beautiful marble dining room, making plans to visit the Taj Mahal the next morning, and Walter slipped this little velvet box across the table.

'Rubies for my ruby on the occasion of our ruby,' he said.

Then that night he went and died in his sleep.

All this talk of journeys this morning – well that was the saddest journey of my life, bringing Walter home. I had him laid to rest in the cemetery near our old house so I could visit whenever I wanted. But since I moved here, well he might as well be half the world away.

There was this priest on the wireless earlier – don't ask me what church, they have all sorts on 'Pause for Thought'.

'Life is a journey,' he said. 'Faith is our map and our soul is the compass.'

Well, that did get me thinking about how far I've travelled through my life. From a tatty terrace to a big posh house. All the way to Australia and back – almost to the Taj Mahal. When I married Walter, my world grew and grew, all filled up with places and people. Then, when he'd gone, it shrank right down again, until it's ended up no bigger than this bungalow. Until even a trip to Tescos is too big an expedition for me. As for this wedding Michael and Annie are planning in California – that's too far for me these days.

After I had that dream about Walter, I woke up crying. I wanted so much to go with him, but I was frightened. Like after he died when I didn't leave the house for months. Then this morning, pinning on that ruby brooch, it just took my breath away.

So now I'm sat here, looking out the window at the snow. I've got Walter down from the mantelpiece to keep me company. The opera house picture and one of him in his RAF uniform – so smart and handsome, in a nice silver frame. And I wonder, if I close my eyes and hold him tight.

I'm ready for the next part of the journey, Walter. Let's fly. Let's fly away.

Wendy's Tiger

Wendy Kelly had a Tiger. A real one, not a toy or a moth-eaten old rug. Nor did it have a cute name, it had a proper foreign sort of name, with a 'Boora' and a 'Chicroo' in the middle, not that Wendy had ever seen it written down. Wendy's Tiger spent quite a lot of time in her garage, in case of visitors. Of course, when they were alone, the Tiger had the run of the house. Wendy sometimes worried that the Tiger got lonely in the garage, but knew that he appreciated the reason behind it. If he was spotted, somebody would be bound to call the RSPCA – or the police. After all, not everybody would understand about a Tiger living in a semi in Muswell Hill.

The Tiger just turned up one evening. It was a warm August night and Wendy had left the French windows open. She went into the kitchen to make a sandwich and when she came back, there was the Tiger, lying in the doorway, half in the garden and half in the lounge. Wendy's first instinct was to run back into the kitchen, shutting the door behind her, but something in the Tiger's manner made her stop and think. He looked so relaxed and content and not at all hungry, and she noticed that he was looking at the television. The Tiger was watching an old Carry On film and smiling to himself. He hadn't even noticed Wendy, so she edged her way back into the lounge and sat down quietly on the sofa.

As she started to eat her sandwich, Wendy felt the Tiger look up at her. Nervously she held out her plate to offer the other half, but the Tiger didn't want it. He didn't say 'No thank you' or shake his beautiful head, but he let Wendy know just the same. And he was such a Wonderful Tiger. Wendy could only gaze and gaze, half in fear and half in admiration. The Tiger paid no attention, he just lay there watching the old film and smiling to himself. Gradually, Wendy's fear faded, and she began to smile too. When the film finished, Wendy asked 'Did you enjoy that, Tiger?' and the Tiger seemed to answer yes.

In the weeks that followed, Wendy discovered that the Tiger was very fond of films, with a particular liking for vintage British comedy. He seemed to prefer Black and White to Technicolour, and Wendy agreed that, Yes, she also found Black and White films more atmospheric and, No, they certainly didn't make them like that anymore. As the summer slipped away and the nights became cooler the Tiger would allow Wendy to curl up against him, and his fur was softer than the softest, plumpest cushions and warmer than the warmest, thickest blankets.

Wendy never fed the Tiger in the house. Every evening, as soon as it was dark, the Tiger went out of the French windows and stayed out for an hour or so, always returning before bedtime. When he went out, he looked hungry – when he came back, he did not. Wendy never asked where the Tiger went, because she didn't want to know. She wanted the Tiger to stay with her forever. As there hadn't been a spate of grisly murders or mysterious disappearances from the neighbourhood, Wendy assumed that the Tiger went further afield on his evening excursions.

Autumn was Wendy's favourite time of year, all the more so now that it reminded her so much of her new friend – not that the splendour of the turning leaves could match the Tiger's glorious coat. Wendy often wished that she could take the Tiger for a walk, perhaps to Highgate, or on Hampstead Heath. Not on a lead, you understand, she would never try to tame the Tiger, but it would have been nice just to walk side by side, like friends out for a stroll, and to admire the season together. Wendy would have liked to be able to compare the autumn leaves to the Tiger's coat. Perhaps the Tiger would become kittenish and chase the leaves – he sometimes played games with Wendy, but those were more like wrestling games than chasing games, although the Tiger was careful not to be too rough and always kept his claws velveted. Still, Wendy knew that they couldn't really go for a walk together. After all, not everybody would understand about a Tiger living in a semi in Muswell Hill.

Some evenings, Wendy went out with the people from the office. She didn't have many friends, finding it hard to mix because she was rather shy, but, if a group of people were going out after work, she would often tag along. Wendy was happier in a group, nobody expected too much of her and she could sit and listen to their conversation. She liked to listen because they had such interesting things to say, whereas everything she said sounded silly or dull. Lately, she had wondered what the others would think if they knew about her new friend. But she couldn't tell them – they'd say she was going nuts or, that she'd had too much to drink. After the outings, Wendy would go home and tell the Tiger about the evening: about the pub or restaurant or bowling alley she had been to, who had been there and what had been said. Once the group went to the cinema, but the Tiger was not pleased to hear about that. He seemed jealous and hurt that Wendy had gone to see a film without him, so she never went again. Instead, she searched the charity shops for DVDs and they watched them together.

It wasn't really a hardship to say nothing about the Tiger. Wendy was naturally rather quiet and, although the people at work spoke to her quite a lot, they didn't really listen. But things began to change on the day that the new salesman arrived. His name was Alan and he took a real shine to Wendy. Although he was handsome and older and much more self-assured, he asked her to help him find his way around. Wendy was happy to help; she had become more confident since the Tiger came to stay, although she'd hardly noticed it herself. So, Alan took Wendy out to lunch that first week and she told him all about the office and the people – and how it really wasn't so bad once you got used to it. And on the way home that evening, Wendy realised that she had done all the talking and it had been Alan who had listened. Wendy told the Tiger all about it and the Tiger purred with approval as she stroked his ears.

One evening, Wendy invited Alan home to dinner. She'd discussed this with the Tiger who had agreed to be out of the house as soon as it was dark and not to return to the house until Alan had gone home – Wendy would open the French windows as a signal. If the Tiger felt cold, he would wait in the garage. Dinner went very well; Wendy was a good cook and had chosen a simple but tasty pasta dish for the main course with apple crumble for dessert. Then they settled down in the lounge and Wendy asked Alan if he would like to watch a film. But Alan was only interested in action films with car chases and stars like Tom Cruise or Vin Diesel, although he did say that Wendy's collection of Ealing comedies was 'very sweet'. So, they listened to music on Alan's mobile phone and cuddled up on the sofa, and Wendy soon found that they could have a very interesting evening without watching a film at all.

It was with a strange mixture of desire and self-conscious embarrassment that Wendy allowed herself to be seduced. It wasn't very successful, but Alan told her not to worry, as it often wasn't the first time. Lying on the sofa, Wendy wished she was a smoker, the occasion seemed to call for that – and it would give her something to do with her hands. To preserve some dignity, she got dressed and went out to the kitchen to make coffee. She thought that it was strange, although they should be closer than ever, how distant and uncomfortable she had begun to feel.

When Wendy walked back into the lounge, Alan was standing by the French window, dressed and looking very handsome and safe again. He started towards her to help with the cups.

'It's all right, I can manage.' Wendy said brightly, not wanting him too close again too soon.

He turned back to the window, saying something about the room being stuffy, and, before Wendy could stop him, Alan had opened the doors to the garden.

'No!' Wendy called out, 'False alarm!' But the Tiger was already in the doorway. Alan's face went very white and he backed away against the wall, his mouth opening and shutting although no noise came out.

The Tiger and Wendy looked at each other, and the Tiger seemed to say that he was sorry, but he thought he'd seen the signal.

'It's all right,' said Wendy, sadly, 'It isn't your fault, I know.' But what, she thought, am I to do about it now?

The Tiger sat in the doorway as he had on that first night. Wendy knew that she would have to decide between the two of them. She could either have Alan, or the Tiger; she couldn't keep them both. If it had been an imaginary or a toy tiger, it would have been all right; Alan might even have thought it 'Sweet'. But it was a Real Tiger. That was the problem and the beauty of it. A Real Tiger who had been her friend for months now. She couldn't expect Alan to keep quiet about something like that. Either Wendy must tell the Tiger to go, or lose Alan forever. He would never understand about a Tiger living in a semi in Muswell Hill.

Wendy's thoughts spun round in circles. She saw herself in a few years' time, in a beautiful detached house, the front garden swept and tended with tubs of flowers and honeysuckle growing on a trellis by the door. Her handsome husband walking up the path promptly at six o'clock as she was putting the final touches to his supper. The hall full of adorable, adoring children waiting for Daddy, jostling to show him their drawings from playschool or their glowing Maths reports. And Wendy herself, content in her lovely home with her lovely family and Alan so admiring and devoted to her. He had always been so respectful, and attentive – except for just now, on the sofa of course.

Then she thought of the long winter evenings watching films with the Tiger, her face buried in the thick silky fur, chuckling as Kenneth Williams struggled in Matron's clutches, or Alec Guinness 'Fell to earth in Berkley Square'. Wendy looked from Alan to the Tiger and from the Tiger to Alan and she gave a big sigh.

'It's all right, Alan, I'll take care of this.' Wendy spoke with a voice of new authority. 'I'll explain it all tomorrow. Just promise me that you won't talk to anyone about it till then.' She led him gently past the Tiger who lay sadly, but obediently, with his head on his paws. 'Just tell me that you trust me, and that you won't say a word to anyone until I explain it all to you tomorrow.'

Alan nodded nervously, and Wendy helped him on with his coat and saw him to the front door.

The Tiger was waiting when Wendy came back into the room. 'I had to do that, Tiger, he was so frightened,' she said, 'and, besides, people from the office knew that he was coming here tonight. It's about a twenty-minute walk to the station. You've just got time.' The Tiger got up off the floor and shook his beautiful coat, turned and smiled at Wendy, then stretched his muscles ready for the chase.

After the Tiger had gone, Wendy sorted through her DVDs, arranging them in alphabetical order as she selected a special favourite. They would watch it together when the Tiger got home. There would be quite an upset at work tomorrow; no doubt the police would be involved. But nobody would suspect Wendy. As she'd seen Alan off at the door, Mrs Granger from down the road had called goodnight and stayed chatting as he walked off. Mrs Granger had watched him go as Wendy told her all about her handsome new boyfriend, who worked in sales. Wendy had an alibi. And, besides, nobody would ever guess what had happened to Alan. After all, nobody would believe there was a Tiger living in a semi in Muswell Hill.

(Wendy's Tiger was first published in Good Housekeeping in 2002 after winning their annual short story competition. I've made some slight changes to bring it up to date. JH)

Author's Note

This book is not the book I had intended to write next. It came together by accident.

After I published *The Woman Who Never Did*, I wanted to develop the idea of linked short stories by writing a series of twelve individual, but interlocking, tales that would together comprise one bigger, all-encompassing, narrative. That was two years ago and, to date, I've only managed to complete one of the stories.

In the meantime, a number of kind people had asked me when I would be publishing my next book. I kept replying that I hadn't had time to write it because I've been too busy with family life and other literary projects: festivals, open mic events, even radio. Eventually, I realised I'd actually been writing all the time, albeit not the book I'd intended.

Women in Shorts is a grouping together of short stories (some of them very short, bordering on Flash Fiction) and monologues that were mostly written for open mic and sundry live events. I've added in a couple of other pieces, including *Wendy's Tiger* (originally published in Good Housekeeping), that seemed to fit the theme of the inner life of ordinary women. I've also included one story that isn't written from a woman's point of view, *Monty and Jules*, because I thought it was a good fit with the other pieces in the collection.

The style of *Women in Shorts* is different from that of my first book, *The Woman Who Never Did*. There is no specific link from story to story; in fact, I've deliberately shuffled moods, lengths and ages. However, I maintain that a short story should be Tardis-like in its ability to hold entire human lives within a limited wordcount and I hope you enjoy the lives of the women in these shorts.

If you would like to find out more about my writing, please visit www.jeneferheap.wordpress.com.

Acknowledgements

Once again, I owe a great debt of thanks to you both, Catherine White and Sophie Whitley-Flavell, for patiently reading every single word of my stories (often many times over) and always making time in your very busy lives to give me honest and constructive feedback. Also thank you to Philippa Mitchell, for being the first to read what I'd thought was the final version and helping me tweak it until it really was finished.

Thank you to my editor, Katharine De Souza (www.katharinedsouza.co.uk), for understanding what I'm trying to say and helping me say it in words that are clearer, sharper and more poignant.

Thank you to the readers and audience at the open mic events Upstairs at the Globe in Warwick – many of these stories will be familiar to you, because many were written specifically for those events. Thank you to Alycia Smith-Howard for never failing to over-estimate my abilities and inspiring me to be brave and try really hard not to let you down. And thank you to all the other writers I've met at festivals, literary events, courses, and other places. Your talent and your generosity of time and spirit is such an inspiration.

A special thank you to Kate, Molly (the younger), Sue, Hen, Hannah, Kitty and Molly (the elder) for putting on your shorts and patiently standing in a field with me while our menfolk took photographs. A whole family of women in shorts – I am very, very proud of you all. Thank you to Colin for taking the 'winning' photograph, to Kitty for helping prepare it for the front cover, and to Jim for finding something else to do so your sister could use the family computer. Also thank you to Mike Long (www.hi-pix.com) for the professional (and rather more fetching) photograph on the back cover and to Colette Long for letting me use your wifi when our router crashed at the worst possible moment.

Last, but very far from least, thank you to all my family and friends who continue to help and support me. Thank you for buying my books, writing reviews on Amazon and Goodreads, coming to my events – and for making your family and friends do the same! It means a huge amount. You know who you are and you are all very special.

Made in the USA
Columbia, SC
23 November 2017